NICK BRUEL

A NEAL PORTER BOOK
ROARING BROOK PRESS
NEW YORK

For all teachers everywhere

Page 83, *The Battle at Bunker's Hill*, George Edward Perine after John Trumbull, courtesy of Emmet Collection, Miriam and Ira D. Wallach Division of Art, Prints and Photographs, The New York Public Library, Astor, Lenox and Tilden Foundations

Copyright © 2013 by Nick Bruel
A Neal Porter Book
Published by Roaring Brook Press
Roaring Brook Press is a division of Holtzbrinck Publishing Holdings Limited Partnership
175 Fifth Avenue, New York, New York 10010
mackids.com
All rights reserved

Library of Congress Cataloging-in-Publication Data
Bruel, Nick.
Bad Kitty school daze / Nick Bruel.
    p. cm.
Summary: "When Kitty's owners have finally had enough of her bad behavior, it's time to ship her off to obedience school" — Provided by publisher.
    ISBN 978-1-59643-670-1 (hardback)
[1. Cats—Fiction. 2. Pets—Training—Fiction. 3. Humorous stories.] I. Title.
    PZ7.B82832Bao 2012
    [E]—dc23
                                                          2012015359

Special Book Fair Edition ISBN 978-1-59643-934-4

Roaring Brook Press books are available for special promotions and premiums. For details contact: Director of Special Markets, Holtzbrinck Publishers.

First edition 2013
Printed in the United States of America by RR Donnelley & Sons Company, Harrisonburg, Virginia
1 3 5 7 9 10 8 6 4 2

• CONTENTS •

•CHAPTER ONE•
ONE FINE DAY

11

Oh, dear! What happened, Baby? Did you fall down? How did that happen?

The cat did this? Well, I'm not surprised. Tsk, tsk, tsk. The way those two were running and horsing around. But I'm sure it was an accident.

Kitty, it's time for us to have a little talk.

KIDDY!

Kitty, I've had enough of your SCREAMING and HISSING and FIGHTING. It's time we did something about your behavior, your nasty temper, and the fact that you never seem to listen.

And that goes for you too, Puppy. That drooling problem of yours started all of this.

That's why I've decided it's time for both of you to go to . . .

SCHOOL.

CHAPTER TWO

THE NEXT FINE DAY

HEY, KITTY! I just got back from the store, and look at all of the super-cool school supplies I bought for you! They all feature your absolute FAVORITE . . .

Love Love Angel Kitten

Love Love Angel Kitten
Backpack

Love
Love
Angel
Kitten
Notebook

Love Love Angel Kitten
Eraser

Love Love
Angel Kitten
Pencils

Love Love
Angel Kitten
Bowling Ball

Pinkish
Pink

Reddish
Pink

Deep Pink

Light Pink

Pink

Love Love
Angel Kitten
Crayons

Love Love Angel Kitten
Calculator

Love Love
Angel
Kitten
Gym Shorts

Love Love
Angel Kitten
Tractor
Tire

Love Love
Angel Kitten
Cinder Block

Love Love
Angel Kitten
Ruler

Whew! That's a lot of
stuff! Oh well . . .
Let's put it all into
your backpack.

Awww, look at you! All ready for school.

And so is Puppy! Did you pack your bandana, Puppy? I hope so, because you'll need it if you start drooling again.

We better hurry. You guys don't want to be late for the school bus!

HERE IT COMES!

UNCLE MURRAY'S FUN FACTS

WHY DO DOGS CHASE CATS?

Hey, don' blame the dog for this!

Dogs don't just chase cats. They chase lots of things, because that's what dogs like to do most.

Herder dogs like border collies are bred to chase sheep and keep the flock together. Hunting dogs like hounds and dachshunds are bred to chase foxes and rats. Police dogs like German shepherds are trained to chase criminals. And dogs chase all of these things not just because they like to do it, but also because

they're so very, very good at it.

When a dog chases a cat, it's not chasing because it's being mean. It's chasing the cat because of instinct. "Instinct" is that part of an animal's brain that controls how an animal is going to act. Birds can fly because their instinct

MEOW*

*Albert Einstein once said that "Peace cannot be kept by force; it can only be achieved by understanding."

24

tells them how. Fish can swim because their instinct tells them how. And dogs chase other animals because their instinct tells them it's an important thing to do.

So when a dog sees a strange cat for the first time, his brain tells him that he MUST begin chasing the cat. It doesn't help that dogs are also very territorial, which means that if the cat is anywhere near something the dog thinks he owns, like his bone or his backyard or his house or even YOU, then he will feel compelled to chase that poor cat away.

Cats, by the way, have the same instinct as dogs. Cats are extremely good at chasing other animals, only they chase animals much smaller than they are, like mice and rats. Most dogs are bigger, sometimes MUCH bigger, than cats. So cats do not generally chase dogs.

I like dogs, but they better not chase my school bus!

Dogs, however, do not have the same sense of caution as cats and will often chase things much, much bigger than them. That's why they'll sometimes chase cars.

All right, ya goofy cat, move on to the back of the bus and you can meet some of your new classmates!

27

Bye, Kitty! Bye, Puppy! I'll see you at the end of the day!

•CHAPTER THREE•

WELCOME

All right, you guys! Everybody off the bus and welcome to . . .

35

Well, pets, my name is Diabla von Gloom. But I want you all to call me Miss Dee. Welcome to my school! School, as you may know, is a place where you go to learn something new. So, I really hope that you all learn something new today.

Let's step into the classroom! And as you all head inside, I want you to understand one thing . . .

41

CHAPTER FOUR

CIRCLE TIME

Circle time is how I get to know all of you, and for all of you to get to know each other.

Go ahead, Petunia.

I hate cats.

I just hate them! I hate them so much! I hate their eyes! I hate their noses! I hate their goofy-looking whiskers! When I see them, I just want to punch them!

PUNCH!

PUNCH!

PUNCH!

I . . . I . . . just want to bite their heads off and chew their faces like gum! CHEW! CHEW! CHEW! I want to pick them up and throw them all into active volcanos!

49

I hear ya,
cow sister.

It's your turn, Puppy, but I can't imagine what problem a sweet little puppy dog like you could ever have; although I wonder what we can do about that little drooling problem of yours.

No one tells Dr. Lagomorph, mutant supervillain extraordinaire, that he can't go first. It's just not fair. I'll bet that accursed Captain Fantasticat put her up to this.

61

Okay, then. You don't have to answer the question if you don't want to, but that does not give you the right to be rude to me.

When you're ready to tell me why you're so angry, I'll be listening.

65

Stop blaming dogs! This is all the fault of goofy cats!

UNCLE MURRAY'S FUN FACTS

WHY DO DOGS AND CATS HATE EACH OTHER?

The problem between dogs and cats isn't so much that they hate each other . . . they just don't understand each other. Let's think about how dogs and cats are different from each other.

NOSE— SNIFFS EVERYTHING

TONGUE— LICKS YOU BECAUSE HE LIKES YOU

TAIL—WAGS WHEN HAPPY

Dogs are very social. They live in packs and usually enjoy the company of other dogs. Dogs like to play by wrestling and biting. When a dog first meets you, he likes to sniff you (especially in places where you may not like to be sniffed). When a dog likes you, he expresses it by licking you. When a dog is happy, he wags his tail.

Cats, on the other hand, are not social animals. They lead independent lives and usually do not seek the company of other cats. Except for when they're young, cats do not play with each other and especially not by wrestling or biting. Cats don't sniff things nearly as much as dogs. Cats generally only lick themselves, and then only to clean themselves. And cats only shake their tails when they're feeling nervous or angry.

TAIL—SHAKES WHEN NERVOUS

NOSE—USUALLY ONLY SNIFFS TO SENSE DANGER OR SAFETY

TONGUE— ONLY LICKS HERSELF

Now imagine what happens when a strange dog and cat meet for the first time. The dog runs up to the cat with its tail wagging, expecting to sniff her, lick her, and play with her. But the cat meanwhile sees the dog's running as an attack. She sees the wagging tail as a sign of anger. And the last thing the cat wants is to be sniffed (especially in a place where she doesn't want to be sniffed), licked, and played with. So the cat either runs away or attacks, neither of which the dog expected.

Okay, so maybe the dogs are just kinda sorta partly to blame.

So now the dog has a perception that cats just *aren't* friendly. This isn't going to encourage the dog to be friendly with any cats in the future. And so begins a cycle of misunderstanding that can sometimes lead to a real mess.

•CHAPTER FIVE•
ARTS + CRAFTS

I want each of you to make me something that depicts what you're thinking about right now!

Once it is complete, I shall use it for performing dark and hideous experiments. Perhaps I will give it life! Yesss . . . LIFE! I shall build an entire army of evil Captain Fantasticat clones who will exist only to serve me in my fiendish goal to rule the entire world!

THERE! It is done! Soon the whole world will tremble before my army of evil clones as they sweep across the planet conquering each town, city, and country one by one! No one will be shown mercy from my wrath, for my cruelty will be infinite!

It's very nice.

Thank you.

Hmmm . . . I'm not too sure what to make of this, Petunia. But I do believe we have to find a way for you to make peace with cats.

Wait . . . are you . . . are you giving this to me?

•CHAPTER SIX•
SHOW + TELL

I want each of you to SHOW me something that's special to you and then TELL me why it's important.

95

Well, I . . . uh . . . made two paintings in Arts and Crafts that I want to show you.

This is the first one. It's . . . uh . . . still a bit wet.

Okay, Puppy. It's your turn! What are you going to show us?

Wait! Where are you going, little puppy?

Oh, I see. You found a recorder you want to play.

Well, we're all looking forward to hearing you play it!

Partita in a minor
for Solo Flute

J. S. Bach
BWV 1013

Allemande

CHAPTER SEVEN

STORYTIME

Gather around, everyone! It's been a long day, and I think it's time for us to all sit back and hear a story with a very important message.

Today's story is "Love Love Angel Kitten and Her Friends on the Farm."

One day, Love Love Angel Kitten decided to go visit the farm.

"Oh, what joy that would be," said Love Love Angel Kitten to herself. "I've never met any farm animals."

"And it's always so very, very fun to make new friends!"

So she stepped into her magic rainbow helicopter made out of candy and . . .

But you're not just plain ol' Kitty anymore, are you?
No, now you're . . .

LOVE LOVE ANGEL KITTY!

HEY, EVERYBODY! Look at Love Love Angel Kitty!

She made dinner for us! She's so very, very KIND!

She bought us all presents! She's so very, very GENEROUS!

She cleaned her own litterbox! She's so very, very HELPFUL!

Love Love Angel Kitty is such a very, very, good, good, GOOD Kitty! Look at how much she loves Baby!

—Awww!

Now look at how much she loves Puppy!

Finally, there is peace in our home. Where once there were screaming temper tantrums, now there are only kisses. Where once there were fights and shrieks and howls, now there are only hugs. Where once there was only mayhem, now there is only love. Sweet, wonderful LOVE.

LA-LA-LA-LA-LA-LA-LA-LA

CHAPTER EIGHT

GRADUATION

Well class, this has been a very full day. But it's time for graduation. Do you remember what I told you school is for? School is where you go to learn something new.

This means that if you can show me that you've learned something new today, then I will give you a diploma to show that you've graduated. And then you can go home happy and proud to know that you will all be better pets.

119

FIRST, I HAVE LEARNED THE MYSTIC SECRETS OF TRANSFORMING MY ENEMIES INTO TWENTY-POUND BLOCKS OF GORGONZOLA CHEESE BY USING THIS ANCIENT CRYSTAL I FOUND HERE INSIDE THIS CHAMBER OF LEARNING! I WILL USE IT TO FINALLY DEFEAT THAT DESPICABLE DO-GOODER CAPTAIN FANTASTICAT AND HIS MINISCULE SIDEKICK POWER MOUSE. THEN NOTHING SHALL STAND IN THE WAY OF MY COMPLETE AND TOTAL WORLD DOMINATION!

Well . . . umm . . . I guess I also learned that people will pay more attention to me if I don't interrupt them, even though I'm trying to get their attention.

Well said, little bunny. Here's your diploma!

YAY!

OH, HOW WRONG I HAVE BEEN! I HAVE WASTED SO MUCH TIME HATING CATS WHEN I SHOULD HAVE BEEN LOVING THEM AS I DO MY NEW BEST FRIEND!

OOF—

FROM THIS MOMENT ON, I SHALL DEDICATE MY LIFE NOT TO CHASING OR BITING OR CHEWING BUT TO LOVING THESE KINDEST AND GENTLEST OF ALL THE EARTH'S CREATURES. NEVER AGAIN WILL I SPEAK ILL OF YOU BEAUTIFUL BEASTS. THIS I VOW!

I watched you help your
puppy friend with his
drooling problem.

I watched you be the first
to support the little bunny
with your applause.

I watched you give Petunia
your painting and make
a new friend.

Do you want to know
what I learned about
you today, Kitty?

I learned that you're not such a bad kitty, after all.

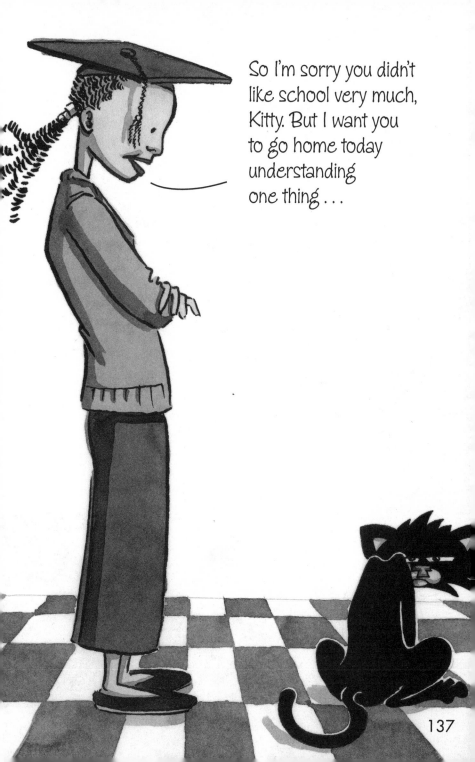

So I'm sorry you didn't like school very much, Kitty. But I want you to go home today understanding one thing . . .

139

Never!

CAN DOGS AND CATS EVER BECOME FRIENDS?

Dogs and cats can and will become friends, but they can't do this by themselves. They'll need your help. The key is PATIENCE. Helping your pets to get along could take a long time and will require a lot of your attention.

MEOW?

First, take a few precautions. Trim the claws on your cat. Put the dog on a leash. Make sure the cat has a place to hide or escape if things get out of hand. And keep some treats on hand . . . you'll see why in a moment.

If you're bringing a cat into the home, keep her in her carrier and let the dog sniff the cat through the air holes. If the dog is calm, give him some treats as a reward. If he barks or is excitable, pull on the leash and tell him "NO" until he calms down.

ARF?

142

If you're bringing a dog into the home, also keep the dog in a cage if you can, at first. Bring the cat into the room by carrying her and petting her to let her know it's okay. If your cat gets wiggly or runs, don't punish her for being understandably anxious. Just pet her and console her.

Another tactic you might try is to keep both animals inside their respective carriers and place them

both in the same room with their doors facing each other. You should stay in the room, too, if only to give them both treats when they are calm. If either of your pets continues to be anxious about the situation, you should be prepared to keep them separate from each other the best you can and repeat this process each day for as long as it takes.

In time, you should be able to train each pet to think of the other as another member of the family . . . an annoying member, perhaps, but part of the family nonetheless.

SIGH—I already have a lot of annoying members of my family.

•EPILOGUE•

Well, Kitty, I'm pretty disappointed with you that you didn't graduate. I can't help but think that maybe you just didn't try hard enough.

SIGH And I guess this means that you're the same old, cranky, ornery, disagreeable Kitty you've always been.

Your teacher Miss Dee kept telling me how much she likes you and how much she hopes that you'll be able to go back to school for another chance. She seemed to really like you, Kitty. But I don't know. I just don't see any reason to send you back to that school . . .

unless we really, really, REALLY have to.

KITTY!

POW!

BLAM

IS THERE A REVERSE SETTING ON THAT THING?

IF ONLY YOU USED YOUR 000 POWER FOR GOOD INSTEAD OF EVIL!

WHY?

WELL... THINK ABOUT IT. YOU'D MAKE A FORTUNE!

REALLY?

SURE. YOU COULD TURN ALL SORTS OF JUNK INTO CHEESE LIKE OLD TIRES, SOCKS, BANANA PEELS. AND THEN YOU COULD SELL THE CHEESE!

HMMM

HOW ABOUT YOU MAKE A RAY GUN THAT TURNS CHEESE INTO MICE!

HA!

HEY!

4

GREAT! NOW YOU BROKE IT!

YAY! I'M BACK!

BING!

CURSES! I SHALL HAVE TO MAKE GOOD MY ESCAPE!

HEY! WHERE DID DR. LAGOMORPH GO?

BEATS ME!

HEH HEH HEH

I DON'T THINK WE'VE SEEN THE LAST OF THAT FIEND!

GOSH

THE END?

I think I need more muscles.

You have enough. Now hush!

What does "subterranean" mean?

Don't miss BAD KITTY's picture books!
MEOW!

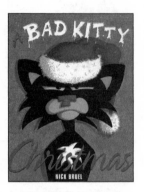

Bad Kitty
ISBN 978-1-59643-069-3
$16.99 US/$18.99 CAN

Poor Puppy and Bad Kitty
ISBN 978-1-59643-844-6
$16.99 US/$18.99 CAN

A Bad Kitty Christmas
ISBN 978-1-59643-668-8
$15.99 US/$18.50 CAN

ABOUT THE AUTHOR

NICK BRUEL is the author and illustrator of the phenomenally successful Bad Kitty series including the 2012 CBC Children's Choice Book Award winner *Bad Kitty Meets the Baby*. Nick has also written and illustrated many other picture books including *Who is Melvin Bubble?* and *Bob and Otto*. Nick lives with his wife and daughter in Tarrytown, New York. Visit him at nickbruel.com.

badkittybooks.com
mackids.com

Can't get enough of BAD KITTY?
Read these hilarious companion books!

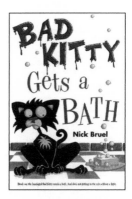

Bad Kitty Gets a Bath

ISBN 978-1-59643-334-1 (hc)
$13.99 US/$15.99 Can
ISBN 978-0-312-58138-1
$6.99 US/$8.99 Can

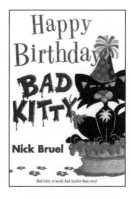

Happy Birthday, Bad Kitty

ISBN 978-1-59643-342-7 (hc)
$13.99 US/$15.99 Can
ISBN 978-0-312-62902-1
$6.99 US/$8.50 Can

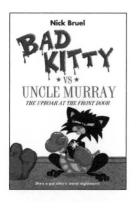

Bad Kitty vs Uncle Murray

ISBN 978-1-59643-596-4 (hc)
$13.99 US/$15.99 Can
ISBN 978-0-312-67483-0
$6.99 US/$7.99 Can

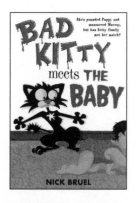

Bad Kitty Meets the Baby

ISBN 978-1-59643-597-1 (hc)
$13.99 US/$15.99 Can
ISBN 978-0-312-64121-4
$6.99 US/$7.99 Can

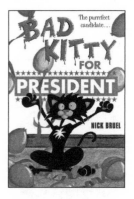

Bad Kitty For President

ISBN 978-1-59643-669-5 (hc)
$13.99 US/$15.99 Can
ISBN 978-1-250-01016-2
$6.99 US/$7.99 Can

badkittybooks.com
mackids.com